Rena Cherry *Brown*

Illustrated by *Mikaila Maidment*

Otter Lee Brave

4880 Lower Valley Road • Atglen, PA 19310

Other Schiffer Books on Related Subjects:

Mother Monarch, 978-0-7643-3400-9, $19.99
Osprey Adventure, 978-0-7643-3684-3, $13.99
Saving Squeak: The Otter Tale, 978-0-7643-3588-4, $14.99

Published by Schiffer Publishing Ltd.
4880 Lower Valley Road
Atglen, PA 19310
Phone: (610) 593-1777; Fax: (610) 593-2002
E-mail: Info@schifferbooks.com

For the largest selection of fine reference books on this and related subjects,
please visit our website at www.schifferbooks.com. You may also write for a
free catalog.

This book may be purchased from the publisher.
Please try your bookstore first.

We are always looking for people to write books on new and related subjects.
If you have an idea for a book, please contact us at
proposals@schifferbooks.com

Schiffer Books are available at special discounts for bulk purchases for sales
promotions or premiums. Special editions, including personalized covers,
corporate imprints, and excerpts can be created in large quantities for special
needs. For more information contact the publisher.

In Europe, Schiffer books are distributed by
Bushwood Books
6 Marksbury Ave.
Kew Gardens
Surrey TW9 4JF England
Phone: 44 (0) 20 8392 8585; Fax: 44 (0) 20 8392 9876
E-mail: info@bushwoodbooks.co.uk
Website: www.bushwoodbooks.co.uk

ISBN: 978-0-7643-4155-7
Printed in China

With love and appreciation to my husband John, my sons, Sam and Jake, and my illustrator, Mikaila, whose talent and spirit made this story come alive.

A tiny sea otter pup scoots in circles above the choppy water,

while his mother forages for food.

"I want to dive to the bottom," Lee chatters, feasting on tasty clams, abalone, and urchins his mother fetches from the sandy bay bottom, "but it's a long way down, and I'm too small."

"You don't have to be big to be brave," his mother says. She cradles her pup on her chest, strokes his sleek fur, and touches his nose with her nose. Lee feels safe and loved.

Suddenly, a dark shadow appears above them. A hungry eagle is soaring toward them. "Lee!" his mother squeals, "dive to the bottom, now!" Without thinking, Lee rockets to the sandy bay floor.

He is so proud to reach the bay floor that he tucks as many clams from the sandy bottom as he can into the fleshy pockets under his arms.

He paddles his webbed feet to the surface to show his mother. He doesn't see her anywhere.

Finally, he spots her under the water—trapped in a fish net! He claws at the netting.

"Go, Lee," his mother signals. "Swim as far away from the net as you can."

Lee tries, but his little paws won't move.

"Sometimes it's hard to be brave, Lee," his mother urges. "Go now!" She touches her nose to her pup's nose through the net.

Lee darts to the surface, and waits for his mother.

Lee bobs all alone until dark.

He clenches his tiny paws above the cold water and blows air into his fur to stay warm the way his mother taught him. He wraps himself with kelp so he won't drift away from their nest. Under a crescent moon and a blanket of blinking stars, the otter pup falls asleep.

For many days, Lee does not play with the other otters.
He never strays far from his kelp bed.

One day, a boat drifts close by.

Before Lee can dive,
a wire cage closes around him.

"Looks like an orphan," says one man. "Don't worry, little one, you'll be at the aquarium before you know it."

The boat carries Lee away, leaving his kelp bed far behind.

Lee moves into a big, deep tank with many other otters.

When he tries to swim away, THUMP! He bumps into a hard wall.

People toss fish from buckets into the water, but when Lee races for the food, a large, sleek otter named Brody knocks him out of the way.

"Too small to fight, little otter?" Brody whizzes past and laughs, as he scoops up the last morsel of breakfast.

Round objects filled with tasty clams and squid float in the tank. Lee bobs at one of the balls with his nose. "Out of the way, tiny tot!" Brody cackles, as he swirls around Lee and knocks the ball up to the rocks.

Sitting alone, Lee watches the waves crash on the rocks in the bay below his tank.

A calm voice says, "Here, little one. Special treat, just for you." The feeder gives Lee abalone from a pail.

"You're here for your protection. These otters have been here since they were little. Not one of them could survive in the wild. Not even Brody."

Before long, a female otter named Trixie starts grooming Lee's fur like his mother used to do.

With Trixie's help, Lee grows stronger every day.

One night, after the lights dim and all goes quiet in the aquarium, there is a loud rumble.

The water in the otter tank swirls around and crashes against the sides. The rocks surrounding the pool tremble, shake loose, and crash into the tank! The lights inside the aquarium flash on and off. Loud alarms scream and blare.

Suddenly, everything goes dark.

Lee and Trixie swim for the rock wall, but it splits away. All the otters cascade over the side of the tank and splash into the cold, dark bay below!

He dives deeper and deeper.

When he surfaces, the open night sky stretches as far as he can see.

He is back in the bay! Maybe he can find his way home.

The otters look back at their aquarium home. The earthquake is making everything on land sway and tumble into the bay.

"Gather in rafts," Lee yells, "or we'll lose our way."

"Don't listen to that little squirt!" grunts Brody.

"We can swim for miles! It's deep here! Watch me dive!"

Brody arches his slick back and disappears under the water.

The otters wait for Brody to reappear.

They wait and wait.

Finally, Brody splashes to the surface.

"See? We should be swimming and diving in the bay, not in a tank."

"Otters!" Lee barks, "The bay is not safe like the aquarium. There is no one here to protect you.

Hook paws together, so we don't drift away. Wait for the people to take us home."

"No way!" squawks Brody, who flips and dances away.

Soon after dawn, a boat putters by.

"There they are!" an aquarium worker yells. "They're hooked together—boys in one raft, girls in the other."

The people toss shrimp to lure the otters close, then, gently put the otters in cages.

"I count fourteen," one man says. "Hey, where is Brody?"

Lee has an idea.

Before the wire door closes on his cage, he slips over the side of the boat.

Lee dives and sees Brody...

...tangled in a fish net, running out of air!

Lee races toward Brody.

Suddenly, he stops.

If Brody is gone, thinks Lee, *he won't toss me out of the way and steal my food, or shove me off the rocks.*

Lee swims in circles and thinks and thinks…

No one knows where Brody is except me. I could leave him in the net.

He is almost back to the boat when he remembers what his mother said: "Sometimes it's hard to be brave."

He knows what he must do.

Lee dives down.

He squeezes his tiny body through the netting and blows air into Brody's mouth. Then he dodges to the surface where he flips around in circles, squealing as loud as he can.

A diver follows Lee and pulls Brody up into the boat.

When they look for Lee, he is paddling farther and farther away.

"Come back, Lee," barks Brody. "I'll give you my clams and squid. You were right. We belong in the aquarium."

Oh, Lee wonders, *do I stay safe at the aquarium, or go back where I belong in the bay?*

Suddenly, Lee hears a litter of young otters chattering on the rocks. A small female otter paddles through the waves toward Lee.

"Go, Lee," Trixie says.

"You have not been away from your home for long.
It is time to be on your own."

Lee's new friend is named Sadie.

That night, Lee brings Sadie a plump, tasty clam.

Before they go to sleep in their new kelp bed, Sadie touches her nose to Lee's nose. "You are so Brave, Lee. Otter Lee Brave!"

Otter Facts

Though the otter is the smallest marine mammal, it is the largest of the weasel family. Adults can be 30-100 pounds.

Otters live almost entirely in the water, eating, grooming, resting, and giving birth there.

Otters can live to be up to 25 years old, though the average life span is 10-12 years.

The otter's fur is very thick, around 1 million hairs per square inch.

The otter's predators include humans, sharks, bears, eagles (otter pups), and killer whales.

By the early 1900s, otters had almost entirely disappeared, killed by humans who wanted to sell their fur.

Otters have returned to healthy numbers. They are now most threatened by oil spills. Oil soaks into the otter's fur and prevents the fur from keeping the otter warm.